Kate and the BIG Cake

written by Anne Giulieri

illustrated by Martin Bailey

"Mom," said Kate.
"We can bake
a cake for Dad."

2

Kate and Mom
baked the cake.

"This cake is BIG!"
said Kate.

Mom looked at the BIG cake.
Max looked at the BIG cake,
too!

"Look!" said Kate.

"Here comes Dad."

"Dad!" said Kate.

"We baked a BIG cake
for you.

Come and see the BIG cake."

9

"Oh, no!" cried Dad.
"This cake is not BIG.
It is little!"

11

"Oh, no!" cried Kate.

"Where is the BIG cake?"

"Look!" said Dad.

"I can see cake on the floor."

"Oh, no!" cried Kate.

"I can see Max.

I can see a BIG tummy, too!"